AF446107

THE
KING'S
VIRGIN.
THE
KING'S
VIRGIN

<u>*PART ONE*</u>

Chapter One

Virginity is a personal thing, I honestly think you don't have to judge anyone on it. Some people willfully looses their virginity and other looses it unwillingly. While some enjoy the moment they looses it, others regrets the moment they looses it. Some looses it through pleasure, while others looses it through pain.

It is a bright summer morning, the sun shines too brightly and reflects it's rays into Diana's room. This wakes the young beautiful servant. She struggles to get up from her bed, because the previous night she was busy with the prince.

She lives in the palace, were she works as the chief maiden to the princess, Princess Annabelle. Diana hails from Damelot . Her father is late and her mother lives in Damelot ,she sells food stuffs in the town. Diana was one of the trusted servant of Late king Duntan.

She gets her towel, ties it over her breast and goes to take a shower.

All and sundry has anticipated this day. It was the coronation of Prince Sillas as the new king of Damelot. It is 7:00am in the morning and the palace was already very busy.

Sanzulloti the head of the knights, directs the palace guards on how the procession would go. He distributes the knights to their respective duty post and urges them to stay vigilant. Message has gotten to the palace two days back that there would be a serious ambush on the kingdom on that day. The palace maids begins the decorations in the palace. The Queen mother of Damelot has made provisions for the materials that would be used to decorate the palace.

The Prince's lieutenant, Kofi goes to wake the Prince from sleep but he got no response. Prince Sillas wasn't present, he had gone to his inner room with one of his female servants.

The prince silence kept Kofi unsettled, he made efforts to know the prince were about. He goes to inquire from the guard at the Prince's entrance, they gives him a negative response. They all assured Kofi that the prince has not come out today.

Diana who just finished from the shower goes to get her costume for the event. On her way back she meets Kofi on the corridor who asked her about the prince were about. She remembers that she saw the Prince yesterday She tells Kofi that the prince was with a servant the previous night. Kofi went out to the Prince's Chambers and check his inner room, he sees the prince sleeping so deeply, he quickly greats the prince.

Long live Prince Silas of Damelot !!

Long live Prince Silas of Damelot !!

Good morning my Lord, it is the day of your coronation and everyone has prepared so much for this day. The prince replied him saying my faithful lieutenant It is a day of joy for the kingdom but I feel so scared also to rule this kingdom. I am just 23 years old and my Father death didn't go well with me.

King Duntan of Damelot was the father of Prince Silas and a Husband to Queen Isabella. King Duntan was a good king during his reign, he was well know for his strength and success at war. The people of Damelot celebrated him so much before his death. He liberated his people for captivity and slavery before his passed away. The kingdom was also called Duntan's land.

Kofi consoled the prince and encouraged him to show strength and courage in his actions, so the people would be able to count on him. The prince comes down and goes to take a shower. He prepares towards his coronation as the new King.

The Prince's sister princess Annabelle, walks into the prince Chambers with her maiden, Diana. She greets him and gives him a kiss on his cheeks. My brother hope you are doing fine! May you live long enough to rule Damelot!! The same greetings comes from her maiden too. Kofi greets the princess and her maiden by making a bow before them both. The prince was startled at the maidens Beauty. She has put on the favorite gown, the one her lover bought for her on her previous birthday. Diana wears a pink décolletage gown which slightly exposes her pointed breast, bringing to light her cleavages. She is really stunning. This got the prince starring so adamantly. Not fully disturbed by the maidens looks, he replies his sister's greetings and asks about his mum's were about.

 Mother is preparing for your coronation and is getting ready for the celebration today. She picks up his princely crown and placed it on his head ,he gets his sword and they all leave the prince Chambers. All has ever anticipated the coronation ceremony. Some people don't witness the coronation ceremony, while some people witnesses one or two. Most the older citizens enjoy that privilege. It was going to be a very big celebration in Damelot. Preparations were put in place by the Royals and the people. They all had anticipated the long awaited coronation, it was a thing of joy for the citizens of Damelot.

Chapter Two

All and sundry are gathered in front of the Palace castle, the walls of the castle is decorated with the prince mural, the castle's flag has been planted around the corners and pinnacle of the castle, Every corner of the kingdom is decorated with ribbons. The drummers are beating the drums and the choristers sings songs of celebration. The palace guards in line with the knights are spotted in specific positions keeping watch of any threat to the celebration.

Shortly, a loud trumpet is heard and the people's attention drifts towards the entrance of the castle. Behold the Prince of Damelot !!!!! The Royal Family then walks out of the castle entrance. Eight knights lead the procession, with the Royal family on a chariot. Diana and Kofi stood at the back of the chariot and behind then is the second set of heavily armed knights whom followed the procession.

The people begins to chant songs of praise to the prince.

Long live Prince Silas of Damelot!!!!!

Long live Prince Silas of Damelot !!!!!

Long live Prince Silas of Damelot !!!!!

The Prince's Entourage processes to the castle square were the ceremony will officially begin.

The Royal family comes down from their chariot and assumes their thrones.

It is the duty of an anointed to crown the prince, so the palace wizard who is a master of sorcery has the responsibility to crown the Prince.

Lokorata the wizard of Damelot comes forward before the crowd and gives the people an opening speech. He says

" Great people of Damelot, we have worked hard all these years to build our peace, our joy, our people, our strength and our land. Today is a great day and one of joy for our people. We have come to pass on the mantle of kingship to the son of our late king, King Duntan of Damelot, we have an obligation to protect our kingdom and this day we swear to protect Damelot with our lives for our children to reap the fruits of our labor. In the light of this may our dear beloved Prince, Prince Silas come forward. The people of Damelot continues to chant. Long live Prince Silas of Damelot!!

Long live Prince Silas of Damelot!!

The prince comes forward and sits on a lower stool. Lokorata the Wizard takes the crown and placed it on Prince and he gets the sword of breath which his father used during war to redeem Damelot from slavery, and blesses the prince with it as he touches his shoulders with the sword. The was a loud sound of trumpet from the choristers showing celebration.

As at this moment, king Silas stands up and addresses the crowd.

"People of Damelot I thank you all for your support and massive love for the kingdom, I wish in a special way to thank the Royal family of the Duntan's land for supporting me. I remember the great deeds of my father and promise to walk in his stead. May his spirit guide me in the journey which I start today, To lead Damelot to greatness. We many never be victims of slavery anymore.

On this day I swear an oath to serve Damelot with my last breath and ensure that safety and longevity of the Duntan's dynasty.

For the love of Damelot !!!!!!!!!!!

For the love of Damelot !!!!!!!!!!!!

For the love of Damelot !!!!!!!!!!!

Thank you grate people of Damelot !

Immediately after the king's speech, there was jubilation in the kingdom, the people begins to chant, long live the King Silas of Damelot.!!

Long live king Silas of Damelot!!

Long live king Silas of Damelot!!

The celebration continues as the people had a lot to drink and eat. The king's entourage proceed back into the castle in the same manner they came. There was to be a huge celebration in the castle, and in the whole of Damelot. People of all domain came for the king's coronation were ready to pass a night in Damelot till the end of the celebration.

Chapter Three

The celebration is coming to a close the people of Damelot are having a lot fun some people started getting intimate, some of the palace guards were making love to their wives and some other were making love to prostitutes the people has drank a lot and we're drunk. Diana the princess Assistant takes permission from her mistress and goes to see her Boyfriend Nathan. Nathan is the son of a peasant farmerin Damelot. He likes to learn his father's profession and helps his father at the farm. Nathan's mum died long ago due to illness .Diana and Nathan have started dating for a short while, so when Diana got to Nathan's house she was not so convenient to open her legs for him. Nathan was calm and a gentleman, they cuddled their way till they slept off.

There was a man who traveled from afar and decided to take a rest at Damelot because it has become late at night. He was also a wizard , but from a far away kingdom. He was popularly know as the White wizard. He was a strong a strong sorcerer. He decides to pass a night in Damelot and in line with the celebration he decides to take a prostitute for the night. The man goes to castle square we're people are celebrating and approaches a lady who happens to take advantage of the night to make money for her self. She follows the wizard to his apartment and charges him 10 Domanian silver coins. He tells her he had no Domanian currency, that he is on a voyage but promises her to make an exchange tomorrow and pay. She then agrees.

 He started kissing her and slightly cuddles her breast, while kissing her, he places one hand on her buttocks and clings it together with his hands. Her sexual tension increases and he could feel it in her veins, her blood vessels had rapidly run through her body. She takes off her gown and throws it on the floor. He is astonished by the shapes of her breast for they looked like water melon. They were extremely large and pointed. He pushes her to his bed and sucks her nipple so aggressively. He pulls his garment and slightly takes off her panties. Oh!!!! how amazing that could be!

 After sleeping with prostitute he tells her that he is a wizard but not in any shock because she has slept with different kind of men. The wizard tells her that a servant would rule Damelot.

"Oh my little lady, I see today is your king's coronation but I say to you that a servant will take up from his stead and rule Damelot.

 The prostitute was amazed at his statement and she decides to use it as a means to extort the wizard. The prostitute tells the wizard that he has committed a very grievous offence by his statements. It was an abomination to speak again the reign of a newly crowned king in Damelot.

 The wizard replies the prostitute, saying ; My magic does not fail me, I am on a voyage to distant land, I have no grudges against your land and your King. The prostitute plays a game on the wizard and increases his pay to 40 Domimian cions. The wizard who is annoyed by the prostitute's actions tells her he has not money on him and that he doesn't have money to give to her. She immediately gets up and in a bid to get favour in return, she hurried to the palace to report the issue to the King. On getting there she meets the palace guards, who questions her intentions to see the King. After much interrogation she was taken to the King. She tells the King all that has happened. The King was worried about it but didn't show it, because the people would see him as a weak King so he immediately orders that the wizard be captured and brought to the palace.

  Kofi, the king's lieutenant leads a dozen of knights to fish out the Wizard. The source of the wizard's magic was sacred and purely for a good purpose so he tried to use him magical powers not to hurt anyone. The wizard knows that he would soon be captured. He got his things ready and embarked on his journey. But Damelot was such a big kingdom that he would take him almost thirty five hours to live the outskirts of the kingdom.

The prostitute takes the guards to the room were she f**ked the wizard but didn't met him there, so they began search for the Wizard. They created awareness that a wizard is wanted, and anyone who has seen this man, should notify the guards.

It was so ironical for a wizard with such power to run for his life. The wizard covers his face with a long robe and sneaks through the Corners of the streets to find his way out. He becomes anxious the moments he sees his face on cards and posters on every wall in the town.

While he is on his escape plan, he meets a crowd and knows that he could not probably take that root, so he went into the woods to take rest and shelter. He pulls down he robe and for that moment he feels the cool air that blows his head. The feels relived a little he decides to take a rest and cools off. While resting at the top of a tree he sees a lady taking her bath in the stream. He looks at her nakedness so adamantly and admires her body from afar. The lady wasn't enlightened on the recent happening in the towns she had come to the stream to take her bath and swim.

Meanwhile, the wizard is still lost in thoughts and barely remembers he is wanted in town. He begins to feel uncomfortable and wanted an affair with the lady. She was really stunning in sight. She barely even knows she is seen by someone. She jumps up and runs naked around the stream, as she jumps up her breast Dangles to different direction. It seems she hasn't enjoyed nature like the way she does by the stream.

The wizard decides to approach her forgetting that he is wanted. He comes down from the tree and walks towards the stream. The lady sights a shadow and covers her breast with her hands. While the remaining part of her body was in the waters. As the wizard approaches, it becomes clear that someone is present. She horridly comes out of the water and grabs her dress, but just then did the wizard come outside and walks up to her. "My lady" he said, how beautiful you look like the Stars of the earth. Good day my love, how is it possible that you swim alone in the stream? Thanks old man, says the lady. The wizard was flattered by the name old man and smiles. He asks if he could join her in the stream she agrees but still didn't allow the wizard to touch her. The lady has made the wizard forget his environment. He was determined to get the attention of the lady. Meanwhile the prostitute and the guards has searched the town and mounted the exist point of the town hoping to get the wizard. The prostitute becomes tired of look for the wizard with the guards, so she lives them and went home to prepare for her sister who has just arrived from the neighboring town, after spending a couple of days there. On getting home, she looks around but does not see her little sister. She asked some other neighbors and they told her that her sister has gone to the stream in the woods to cool off and take her bath. The prostitute decides to join her sister in the stream to cool off, after all she had a long day. She wears her robe a heads to the stream. On getting there she sights a man in the stream with her sister, but is not sure who that might be. So she decided to move further, when she goes closer she sees a cloak on the floor. She recognizes the cloak to be that of the wizard. In order to be convinced she goes do closer and see it is her little sister and the wizard. She wonders how it could be possible that the wizard was in a stream with her sister. Isn't he supposed to be on the run? She asks her self. So that the wizard would not be able to escape the ignores the both and went down to the town to inform the guards. The guards gathers more men and they horridly move to the woods.

 The wizard notices that the birds in the woods started singing and flying out of the trees, then he dawned on him that he was wanted and they must be the people looking for him, he quickly gets out the waters and runs naked to his hide out. But then again he realized that his hide out was not longer the best option. He ran out of ideas but make efforts to still escape. He quickly gets his trousers and robe and in an attempt to make the move he notices a dog, the dog started backing angrily at him. This draws attention to his location. The knights hears the backing off a dog and horrid to the place were they heard the back and caught the wizard trying to escape, they threatened to shoot an arrow to him. He the realized that it was the end. In awe he raises his hands and goes on his knees. The knights ceases him, binds his hands and takes him along with them.

Chapter 4

The palace guards arrives the palace with the wizard, they drags him into the gate of the palace and takes him to king. The King who was worried about the utterances of the wizard, looks up to see the wizard on the floor kneeling before him. He is quite at first, but speaks up afterwards and asks the wizard what he has come to do in Damelot, the wizard speaks up that he is on a voyage to the far kingdom of Hamptiton and so he got exhausted and he decided to take a rest at Damelot, when after the coronation ceremony, he made-out with a certain prostitute when he saw a trance and behold it was your majesty. I shared my vision with her not knowing that she would use it to blackmail me. He said!!

 The King is so interested in the vision in particular, because that is what bothers him most. So he asks the wizard to repeat the same vision he saw to him. The wizard say, "my Lord, that a servant from another kingdom will rule this land is not in my intention for your kingdom but my vision say that so clear. The king asks him we're would the servant come from, the wizard tells the king he doesn't know, he is not certain.

The King told the guards to dismiss the wizard and keep him in a room. The guards weren't ok with the king's decisions but had no choice but to obey the king's orders. They forcefully takes the wizard to the plain room. The plain room in Damelot was a room were people who weren't found guilty were kept for further questioning. The plain room, as the name implies, was very empty and had nothing inside. It can't be compared to the prions cell of Damelot were The prisoners messed up everywhere.

The King requests to see the wizard of Damelot, his lieutenant Kofi rushed out to fetch the kingdom's wizard.

The appointment of the wizard of Damelot is strictly patrilineal. Kofi goes to the cave of the wizard of Damelot, his name is Morgan. On getting there, he greets the wizard of Damelot and enters his cave. They both entered the cave. Kofi tells the wizard that the king wants to see him at the palace. The wizard asks the king's lieutenant hope nothing is wrong. Kofi says it is not serious and they both left to see the king.

In an hour time, they both get to the palace. The King receives the wizard warmly. He tells the wizard of Damelot, that a man who claims to be a wizard has made a prophecy that a servant will rule the kingdom but the servant would come from his linage. He tells the wizard that he is kind of confused and he wants the wizard to give his opinion on it. He explains to his Wizard that he wants him to use his magic to check out the possibility of the prophecy.

Morgan the wizard of Damelot tells the king that looking into the future is a very brawny part of magic. It is difficult to practice and rear to see wizard who can see the future. But he assures the King that he would see what he can do to help.

The king's mother hears about the rumors of the prophecy, in anger she leaves her Chambers and horrid to the King Chambers to ask him about utterances of a so-called wizard, and what he has done about it. The King tells his mother that he is taking things slowly, but he will get to the top of the issue. The Queen mother wasn't really happy with the idea, she exclaims that the wizard must be punished. She leaves angrily.

On her way out, there was a loud noise which came from the town, the head of the Knights Sanzulloti, summons the guards were shocked. They ran quickly to the basement to get their weapons and ran outside the palace, to the scene of the explosion. They found out it was an explosive. The kingdom of pampot has come to reclaim a small land which they had fought for, for years ago during the time of King Duntan. King Duntan made sure he preserved the land for his people before his death. The king of pampot heard about the death of King Duntan and planned an attack on Damelot. Since he knew that the King Duntan's son was much young and has no too much experience. The explosion was planned to give warning to the king that they have come back to get the land back.

Sanzulloti hurries back to the palace and informed the king that their land is unsafe. The explosion came from the knights of the pampot, they had attacked the town as a message to the King that have come to reclaim their land.

   King Silas becomes more nervous, he knows he had to show bravery, he was so worried. He walks about the house wondering what would be his next step. He hears a knock on the door and wonders who was that, in anger he shouted for the person to leave his door. But Diana said, my king it's your servant Diana. Immediately, his nerves becomes calm and he orders her in. She was sent by her mistress, princess Annabella to deliver a special dish which she prepared to him. Diana presents the food before him, he finds it difficult to eat, he apologizes to Diana for scaring her by shouting. She tells the king, my Lord you look down, if I may ask, what may be bothering you? The king tells her that a lot of things are on his mind and that the kingdom is facing threat from external Forces. She consoles the King and tells him that all would be fine. King Silas likes the behavior of Diana, he admires her looks and Beauty. The king has started growing feelings for the servant. It has been going on for quite a while now.

She greets the king and walks out of his Chambers. The king looks at her and admires her looks. He looks at her waist and admires her so dearly. The presence of Diana has calmed the king down.

King Silas, immediately orders Kofi to source for the head of the knights, Sanzulloti. Kofi hurriedly runs out of the chambers, he goes to basement to look for Sanzulloti. They both leave and went to see the King. They meet the king already dressing up for war. He was putting on his breast plate and picks up his sword. He orders Sanzulloti to run and summon the knights and the palace guards, that they we're going for a war. Sanzulloti goes to the Pinnacle of the palace and shakes the bell. When the bell is rang, it is a call to duty . The moment the bell was rang, all knights in the palace went to the get more weapons and gather in front of the palace. They number about 5,000 standing soldiers in numbers. The horse men were present and all were set for the war. Some knights were to stay back and protect the kingdom. They were prepared to launch an attack on the kingdom of

Pampot. King silas address the knights saying. We the people of Damelot will fight to safeguard our land. We will fight to safeguard the interest of our people. We can't be threatened by inferior Kingdoms. We are waging an attack against the people of Pampot and they shall pay dearly for their actions.

We must be strong!

We must be brave!

We must be victorious!

For the LOVE of Damelot!!!!!!!!!!!!!!!!!

The knights repeated it again and again as the matched out of Damelot going for war.

Chapter 5

As they approached Pampot, the knights of Pampot saw them from afar and alarmed the other knights, that their kingdom is under terrible attack. They engaged them in an arrow duel. That marked the beginning of the war. They fought for a long time almost 10 hours the was still on and Damelot had already lost some men, although they were marking success in the war, because they have penetrated the gates of Pampot and were marking a notable success in defeating the soldiers. The King was the leader of the infantry that lead the soldiers. King Silas tells his chief soldiers that they should take another route, to reach the King. Once they are able to capture the King, the war would be over. All the soldiers of Pampot would have no choice but to surrender to them. King Silas, Kofi, Sanzulloti, belloti (knight), sazkay(knight) and five other knight follows them to sneak into the palace, because the resistance from the entrance was too much. They went back and passed round the woods to access the back entrance to the palace. They climbed up the roofs top of some houses and sneaks to the Palace window. They first of all entered a room in the palace and they happened to see an Old woman, one of the knights wanted to strike, but the King holds his hand and orders him to drops his sword and not to harm the woman. The woman begs the King and his knights for her life and pleaded with them not to kill her. The king gave her water to drink and orders the guards to go in search for the King of Pampot, while he takes the woman out to avoid her been killed by the other knight. While the King takes the Old woman to her exist point, the old woman thanks the King for his kind gestures and tells him that his goods deeds must be rewarded. She tells him that his destiny has changed and that the prophecy of the wizard will not come to pass. But she tells the King to come the next week to her cave and she will tell him what he must do. He went back to the war ground, in search of the King of Pampot. The knights of Pampot and their King had went to the basement to fight also. King silas sights the King of Pampot and in addition with his guards, he attacked the king of Pampot. It wasn't easy for the Damelot soldiers to Sundue the knights of Pampot. They had captured the King and are on there way back to Damelot.

As they Return back home, they sing and chants songs of victory. The king is so happy. It was his first war as king of Damelot and he won it. He has wanted to prove his strength by waging war first against Pampot and at last everything went well.

From a distance, heavy trumpets we're heard, war songs were chanted, and from the beats of the drum and the echoes of the songs, it was obvious that the knights of Damelot has returned safely. They had won the war against Pampot.

From a distance, the people of Damelot, welcomes the knights warmly, they play good songs and sings victory songs for Damelot.

When they arrived the kingdom, the king addresses the crowd with confidence at the square. He tells them that they have fought and conquer their enemies. He says, We have defeated our enemies , we have regained freedom, we now have peace in our land. As we grief our falling hero, we celebrate our victory also. They fought for their kingdom and sacrificed their lives at the war front for Damelot. They may continue to remain in our hearts, we won't forget their good deeds.

The king announces that there would be a huge celebration tonight to celebrate their victory against the kingdom of Pampot.

The king of Pampot was thrown inside jail and the knights all went to prepare for the celebration. Celebrations like this in Damelot are usually backed up by sex. The people of Damelot liked have sexual intercourse very often.

It is evening the celebration has started in the palace Hall. All and sundry are present. The knights are drinking and eating, there is too much food to eat and drink for the night. They are dancing and having serious fun with themselves.

The king, his mother and his sister are all present at the Hall. The decides to go to the palace and take a rest, while the rest of the knights were drinking.

King Silas goes up to his Chambers to sleep, when he sees Diana. Going to her Chambers. Initially Oslow Diana's lover has requested that Diana comes to see him that night and she was making preparations for that when the King's approaches her. Diana my princess, says King Silas. Diana greets the king, my Lord.

Do not worry too much, come to my chambers. The king says, She reluctantly follows him to his Chambers.

   Silas followed Diana in her tight pink gown. Just the two of them in a completely empty chambers. Kofi was down stairs in the hall drinking with other knights.

Diana is tall, fair and beautiful she is in her early twenties.

King silas checked Diana's body out at every opportunity, scantily hidden beneath her skin tight pink dress.

Diana and king Silas stood an inch too close together.

King Silas went for it.

Silas stepped towards Diana. She was really not comfortable with it. She had a lover and she to stops King Silas. But it becomes obvious that the king was in the mood for sex and he loves her too. Ever since, he has been looking at her closely. Diana was a virgin, she has never had sex before, It was obvious that king Silas has become drunk.

The couple now stood nose to nose in the empty chambers of the "What are you doing? "Diana could feel silas' breath against her lips.

Diana did not move. The two stood face to face, feeling one another breath. The awkwardness of the moment got to Silas and his lips found and kissed her.

Diana's mouth was soft and sweet. Silas kissed her, opening her sweetness.

pressed his tall body into small Diana and he pressed her up against the wall.

Diana's mouth opened more and more as they kissed, her moist tongue driving him crazy.

Silas kissed Diana face and neck while her hands explored his body silas kept her pinned against the wall, pressing his pelvis into her.

 hands moved down her neck and touched her through her tight pink dress.

"Fuck!!! my Lord, we shouldn't be doing this."

"I Know, have fun don't talk."

Silas hands found the hem of Diana's dress and slid beneath it.

Silas touched Diana's legs and felt the lace of her panties.

Silas touches Diana through a thin layer of lace. Diana cropping silas and stroked him through his trousers.

Diana lowered herself to her knees, unbuttoned his jeans, and took him into her brace mouth. Diana looked up at me, her tongue dancing on my tip, her deep brown eyes looking up from beneath Diana. legs and high-heeled feet splayed out awkwardly as she touched herself and took silas in her mouth.

"Oh my god, that feels so good," moaned.

Encouraged, Diana licked, and sucked, and touched, and teased.

Silas hips churned in and out of Diana body as she looked up at his body. Silas kissed Diana's cheeks and played with her hair.

Diana ribbed herself through her black lace panties.

Von was large in Diana small mouth. She was careful to keep her teeth and braces away, and rely on her lips and tongue.

The couple was awkward due to their differing sizes ands heights, but silas forced his way in anyhow, practically picking up bringing her sex to his.

Diana trembled silas humped in and out of her, her body splayed, her legs awkward in heels. Silas humped desperately into this goofy girl, far driven by an uncontrollable male passion.

The liquids of the couple mixed, their sexes becoming one, one passion.

Silas wrapped his arms around Diana, and led her down onto the rough beige carpet of the floor. They kept their bodies together and arrived on the floor.

Silas playfully pinned Diana wrists down into the rough beige bed.

extended Diana's humps, taking his time, letting the high and euphoria slow down and space itself, Diana loves the feeling, she has never felt that way before. King silas grinds on top of her slowly as he goes in and out of her Virginal. She was not a virgin, she has lost that unintentionally, long ago.

She lost her virginity at a very tender age. While she was much younger, her parents were taken into captivity and were enslaved, they were forced to save their child's life by hiding her in a dark room during the attack, Little Diana at the age of five was saved by her uncle, who took her to his house in the neighboring town and trained her. As time went on, she grew up and started her adolescence. Her breast started becoming bigger than it used to be, her hips became wider, she grew very fast and her buttocks became larger. She had this natural beauty that draws suitors to her at a tender age of fifteen. She became attractive to her cousin brother, Brian who took advantage of his relationship with her to rape her. One faithful morning, Brian's uncle went to hunt for a game, at home was Brian who was twenty years old as at that time and little Diana. He took advantage of the moment and trust she had for him, and called little Diana into his room. She innocently went to his room, he ask her to please help him with water, been obedient to her senior cousin brother, she innocently fetch him some water, as she drops the cup with him to drink, he tells her to come and lay with him, she innocently went to his bed in trust not knowing what would come next. Brian begins to feel Diana's face and body. He moves his hand slowly to her little breast and immediately, she screams aloud, Brian quickly covers her mouth, he tries not to be violent with her, he rips her skirt down and tears her pants apart, she tries to scream but her mouth was tightly covered with his hand. He forcefully inserts his hard cork into her tender pussy, he pushes his cork in and out rapidly, without pity for the little girl. She cries so hardly and bleeds profusely. When he sees her bleeding, he was griped with fear and pulled his cork out. She cries out, but have nobody to cry out to.

Brian knew his father would be so mad at him so he drives her out of the house and told her not to come back home. She cries on the streets until a stranger helped her and rehabilitated her. That day she had lost her virginity unwilling to her cousin, whom she trusted so much.

Brian lied to his father that little Diana can out of the house for the reason that she is not well fed.

   Meanwhile while, Oslow was waiting for Diana to come over to his place, but she has not arrived yet, so he believes that she is busy with something, and he decides to go to bed, and promises to see her the next day.

Chapter 6

It is the dawn of a new day, King silas wakes up, he gets up later than usual because of the stressful day that had just passed and of course because he was fully at work last night. While still on the bed, he recounts the episode he had with Diana the previous night, he was not quite happy for his actions, but he couldn't hide his feelings, he couldn't hide the fact that he liked the experience. He wasn't a virgin though, but he hasn't had sex in a long while. King silas whishes he could do it over and over again with Diana.

He realized that he hasn't seen her and she hasn't come to deliver anymore message from his sister as usual, so he decided to send for her. He immediately sent for Diana, he walks about the his chambers in disdain. The King is under pressure, he is eager to see Diana.

Few minutes later, Kofi arrives with Diana, walking next to him. When the door opens, King silas stares so adamantly towards Diana. Diana greets the king's she usually does. King silas asks how she is doing and tells her to sit on his bed. She walks towards his bed and sit.

Since she came, she has been quite. King silas notices the coldness with which she answers him. He tells her to be relaxed and not to think too much because of the sex episode they had the previous night. He begs her not to deliver the message to anyone, "let this be between us" he said. She agrees to the king's idea, she say she won't make it know.

Diana knew that she has done Oslow wrong, she feels so guilty. Oslow has been very helpful and kind to her, he shows her love and takes care of her. The guilt of sleeping with the King made Diana very much uncomfortable. She decides to tell Oslow about the night she spent with the King. She finds it very difficult to tell Oslow, she was really confused about the whole thing. She did not know who to talk to about it and then, she summons courage to meet Oslow.

Oslow has already planned to see Diana, to make up for the night she couldn't come over to his place.

Diana find out that she was falling for the King, she knows that if she gets married to the king, she would bring a lot of good to her self and family. She would no longer work as a servant at the palace anymore, she thinks about the good things she would benefit from dating the king. In as much as she would not want to offend her lover Oslow, she also want to enjoy the benefits of dating the king. Many young beautiful girls in Damelot would do anything to be in her shoes.

Oslow comes to the palace to see Diana, they both exchange pleasantries and they hug so tight. They both exchange kisses, when king silas came into the corridor. He adjusts his crown and cracks his throat. This is to show that they aren't longer two persons in the corridor, so they should stop the cuddling. King Silas passed and moves to his chambers. He feels jealous about Diana and Oslow, he wish Oslow was not in the way. These past few days after the night he had sex with Diana, he has always wanted to go closer to her. He wanted Diana to be his. This bothers him a lot, he becomes so much on love with his servant.

Meanwhile, Diana follows Oslow out of the palace, they both moves to Oslow's house, Oslow has long anticipated sleeping with Diana, since they

started dating, they haven't had sex.

They gets to the bedroom, Oslow has always anticipated the day he would have sex with Diana, as they gets into the room, they started kissing. Diana takes her mouth to his and sucks his lips. He grabs her soft buttocks and clings his fingers tips under her dress. He touches her panties and feels the little piece of meat between her legs (Clitoris). She immediately becomes wet, she enjoys the feeling, the act puts her fully in the mood she grabs Oslow dick slowly and rubs the tip with her hands.

They starts pulling their clothes, she draws down her dress, Oslow feels her breast, he touches her nipples seductively.

She is so turned on, he takes off his clothes and slowly pushes Diana on the bed, he climbs on her and lay series of kisses on her neck, and draws it down to her breast. He sucks her nipples and put his fingers in her pussy at the same time. She grabs his testicles and romances it. She strokes his dick while he slashes sperm on the bed. She turns backwards and shows him her buttocks. He slaps it in different directions and places his cap into her ass hole, She moans slowly as he drives in and out of her of ass. Her butt is extremely soft. He grabs her butt over and over again with his hands. He swings her to the opposite direction and inserts his dick into her pizza shaped vaginal. He goes in freely and come out freely. He enjoys the feeling. It was like a bomb of fire in Diana's brain. She is getting to orgasm. They both had good sex that Night.

Chapter 7

It is the day the King was to go and see the old woman. He wakes up very early in the morning at about 4:00 am, gets up from the bed and goes straight to the bathroom were he washed his face. He gets his sword and wares a black hoody gown, which goes long down from his head to his toe. He does this to hide his identity. He is dressed up like an assassin.

He quickly rushes to the basement of the palace to get his horse which he was to use to embark on the journey and leaves immediately. He knows the secret hide- out, out of Damelot, so he follows that route to avoid meeting the knights at any point in time. The rushes as much as possible to get to the Old woman cave in time and leave before dawn. He beats his horse to move faster and faster. While he approaches Pampot, which no more exist as a Kingdom because their King has been captured and their army has fallen, he hears some strange noise coming from the woods. He tries to move fast to avoid mishaps, but suddenly some bush men runs out of the woods and starts chasing him. They never had any Idea it is the king of Damelot. They were four in number, they draw closer and closer. King silas could no longer run like a thief anymore, so he comes down from his horse and immediately, the bush men comes down also. They could really see his face clearly, so they ask him to take off his hoody, but he draws out his sword. They looked at each other and starts laughing. They laughs at his actions and the four men draws out their sword also. The King gets so up het, he ran towards the men with his sword on the air. He was ready to fight. The men comes closer and they gets themselves involved in a fight. King Silas has trained so hard when he becomes king he became so strong and powerful in martial arts. He follows up with the bush men, with his special skill he beats them up and binds them together. He then removes his mask and reveals his identity to the bush men. They recognizes king silas and they were all shocked, they beg him to leave them there and apologizes for their actions.

 King silas climbs his horse and continues his journey to the old woman's cave. He moves faster so je won't spend to much time at the old pampot. He finally arrives the fallen gates of Pampot. The sight of the broken pillars and the fallen gates remind him of the episode of the war they fought with the people last week. He recounts his war to the old woman's cave. During the war, he met the woman hiding in the castle, she had given him directions to her cave. He remembers the route to the route and goes to the cave.

 On getting there, the place was very dark and old. He knocks but there wasn't any response, so he enters the cave. Scared by the serenity, coldness and darkness of the cave, he draws out his sword and slowly moves inside the cave. He stops the moment he sees reflections of light from the cave. It was the old woman he has come all the way from his palace to see. She is seated by a small flame of fire which keeps her warm. King silas draws closer to the fire and sees the woman, he keeps his sword and greets the woman. The old woman replies him saying My old friend king silas, you are welcome come sit here. The king draws closer to her and sits, he removes his hoody and rests his sword by the wall. He explains the prophecy of the wizard to the old woman. He is so anxious to hear what the woman has to say is the remedy for the prophecy to be broken. She tells him that he will simply have to marry a virgin girl. King Silas at last has heard a solution to the prophecy, but wasn't convinced. He asks the old woman if this was all, she replies him warmly with a nod. He was confused at that moment. To marry a virgin wasn't such a big task to do. He expected a lot of tasks to be done for the prophecy to be reversed but he gets a minor task. Thank you very much woman for your efforts made. He goes to were he had tied his horse and brings ornaments, fine clothes, food stuffs, royal gifts and 100 pieces of dominian currency. The woman thanks King Silas for the gifts and wishes him safe journey back to his kingdom. It was getting to dawn, the sun was rising already, king silas hurried back to his kingdom, he moves as fast as possible. On getting to the kingdom, he stops at the entrance of the kingdom leaves his horse outside and walks in like a normal man. This was to hide his identity from the people. The couldn't recognize him because he had covered his face with his hoody. He finally finds his way into the palace and he heads straight to his palace. Kofi his lieutenant has seen him leaving the palace very early in the morning and also saw him when he had arrived the palace. Kofi knocks at his door, he said open the door and come in. Kofi comes into the chambers and asks the king were has been? King silas lied about it that he has been present in his chambers. Kofi reveals to the King that he has seen him the moment he left the palace and also saw him when he came back. He convinced King Silas that he can always tell him what the problem is. King silas on his part needed someone to share his story with, but no one was so trusted except for Kofi. He explains his journey to the old woman's cave to his lieutenant and tell Kofi the remedy that was given to him. Kofi was happy that it was a very easy task to do. He tells the king that there is no need to be bothered about it. King silas was happy about the progress he has made. He tells Kofi that he needs to get some rest and food so he goes to sleep. Kofi takes his leave and excuse the king.

Chapter 8

Meanwhile Diana had just spent the night with Oslow her lover. She was still at sleep, when Oslow quickly wakes her up to get ready to go to the palace. She took the bedsheets and covers her breast down to her toes with it. She rushes to the bathroom and washes her face, she quickly gets her panties and clothes and put them on. She gives Oslow goodbye kisses and went finds her way to the palace. She enters her room and gets ready for the day's job.

  The Queen mother, Issabella enters the king's chambers and she meets him still sleeping. She wakes him up. Why are you still in bed by this time of the day? Aren't you not supposed to be awake by this time. It is twelve noon and you are still in bed. The King stretch his body, and manages to get up from the bed. He greets her. I hope there is no problem mother. What brings you mum? She keeps him quite, but goes closer to King Silas. My son you are now the king of Damelot and it would be of importance if you will get a wife for yourself and starts producing children that would take after the throne when you are no more. King silas Tells his mother to relax and be calm. He urged the Queen mother that he will get a wife soon enough. The Queen was delighted to hear that. She now puts on a fine smile on her face. I have a beautiful lady for you. And I am very sure you would find her very interesting. Says Queen Issabella. I do not need any lady, I don't know. I have a woman in mind. When I am ready, I am going to settle down. Queen Issabella leaves the King's chambers and goes to see her friend.

After the Queen Issabella leaves the palace, king silas starts to reason who he is getting married to. He also remembers what the old woman said about him getting married to a virgin girl. He loves Diana very well, he has a very strong feeling for her also. He decided to marry Diana, but Oslow was Diana's lover and he know it won't be easy to marry Diana. He wishes he had met Diana long ago. He begins to wallow in thoughts and imagines how he will get married to Diana and how they are going to have children.

Meanwhile, Diana has been cleaning up and is ready for work. She goes over to the princess's chambers to check up on her. The princess has been long awake and was just playing the flute. She learnt the act of playing the flute from her late father king Duntan. Diana greets the princess and they both discuss and cracks jokes with themselves. Diana was really close to the princess and they both maintained a good relationship. While they were present together in the room, the princess sees an old picture of their childhood. She gives the Diana the picture and tells her to give it to the king. Diana reluctantly left to the king's Chambers.

 At the king's chambers, she knocks on the door, king silas gets up from his bed and went to open the door for Diana. Long live the King of Damelot. Diana says, as she gives the king his picture. The king's holds her back he as she was about to take her leave. He holds her hands and tells her to sit with him. Diana knew the king has started developing feelings for her, she likes the king as well but she was already in a relationship with Oslow an d she wouldn't want to break his heart. King Silas tells Diana how much he loves her, he begs her to please replicate his love for her back to him. The king's confession of love to Diana, throws her off balance. She becomes in a state of dilemma. She still nurses the secret of the night she shared the king's bed with him. She has not discussed her plight with anyone yet.

 Diana wishes Oslow she wasn't in a relationship with Oslow. He is the reason she not accepting the king's love. She says to herself anybody would fight to be in my situation.

Chapter 9

Day after day, the King would send flowers and gifts to Diana. Their love suddenly grew stronger day by day. The king sends gift to her parents in the town. Dian dreams of being the Queen of Damelot.

Days turns into weeks and weeks into months. A lot has changed in Diana's body. She starts feeling feverish, she notices a change in her body system. Diana has become **Two**. She knew that she has become pregnant. Her stomach started expanding. But she tries to conceal it by wearing bigger clothes, most especially gown. It becomes obvious that she was pregnant.

It was dawn of a new day, Diana Wakes up feeling weak. She feels pain all over her body, she becomes heavy day after day, she turns on the shower and washes her body. She takes her hands round her stomach, she feels the increased round structure of her stomach. She begins to imagine the feeling of carrying her own child. She finishes bathing, puts on her dress and goes to see the princess. They greets each other as usual. Princess Annabella looks at Diana in awe, she notices how grown Diana's stomach has become. Diana are you heavy? Diana are you pregnant? She asks again. Diana keeps quite she is short of words. She reluctantly says yes. Princess Annabella is very surprised. She congratulates Diana. Thank you for your concern Princess. Diana begs princess Annabella not to tell anybody about her pregnancy. Princess Annabella assumes the pregnancy is for Oslow so she didn't bother asking Diana.

  Princess Annabella has prepared a delicacy for there brother as she normally does. She usually sends Diana to go serve it to the king. But out of care, for Diana , knowing she was pregnant, decides to serve the king by herself from that moment. She also reliefs Diana from some of her normal duties. Starting from that morning, Princess Diana packages the king's food specially prepared by herself, and takes it to give the king. Princess Annabella knocks on the on the door of the king's cambers. The king orders the palace guards at the front of his chambers to open the door and let the person enter. He notices it is his sister, he greets her. She brings in his dish and presents it before him. He tells her thank you and asks about Diana. He asks Anabelle how is Diana and were she is? This is because it is usually Diana she sends to bring the food. I brought the food today and it will be like that for a while. Diana is heavy and I need her to get some rest. Diana is what ???? King Silas was shocked he asks again, Did you say Diana is pregnant? Yes she is says princess Annabella. She just told me this morning, by the way, haven't you noticed her stomach size? It has increased. Why are you so interested in her? Hope nothing is fishy. No nothing is the problem I just wanted to know. Ok whatever though I am off to my chambers I need to attend to some minor issues. Anabelle leaves king silas' room. Kofi ! Kofi ! Kofi ! King silas shouts Kofi's name. Kofi rushes out to meet King Silas. Here I am my Lord. King Silas order him to go look for Diana and bring her to his chambers as Soon as possible. Kofi leaves as Soon as possible, he goes to look for Diana. He soon sees her talking to some friends who are also fellow maidens like her too. He greets all of them and informs Diana of the request to see her with immediate effect. They leaves the venue and goes to the king's chambers.

 They enters the king chambers, king silas stands up in haste and welcomes Diana. She was surprised at the hastened reception. She could not asks the King any questions so she just complied. King silas excuses Kofi out of his chambers. He asks Diana who is the father of her baby? She tries to pretend she doesn't know what he is talking about. But he insisted and tells her that he knows all about her pregnancy she shouldn't play any games with him. Moved by fear and assurance that the king already knows what she was hiding she tells the king that she is. The king was happy, he jumped up and wonders about the room in joy.

 Diana was a little confused about his celebration, she decided to ask him why he is celebrating, he tells her that he has a child and the is very Happy about it. He believes that this would be a great news to his mother.

 Diana is quick to tell him that she doesn't know the owner of the child. The king's face changes. He was a little confused, he didn't know what else to say. He becomes short of words.

Diana quickly explains to him that she had sex with Oslow her lover a week after the mistake that happened between them.

 King silas becomes angry, he orders Kofi to inform the kingdom's physician, that he should run a pregnancy test on Diana by tomorrow. He was so eager to know who the baby is for. At this point, it has become an open secret that Diana is pregnant and King silas maybe the father.

 She imagines the pain and betrayal that would befall Oslow, if he finds out from someone that she is pregnant, so she decides to go and look for Oslow herself to tell him about it.

 She gets to Oslow's home and knocks on the door. Oslow comes and opened up the door for her. He was very excited that she has come to see him. But he wonders what brings her today. She wasn't looking so happy. She tells Oslow that she has made a grievous mistake. Oslow shows her love and affection. He was really very anxious to her what she has to tell him. Diana tells Oslow that she is pregnant. Oslow was so happy, he immediately started dancing. He begs her to please keep the pregnancy, she assures him that she won't dear to abort her baby. Oslow becomes more happier. Diana didn't know how to tell him that she doesn't know the owner. She summons courage to tell him. She stammers and fumbles but finally speaks. Oslow you shouldn't celebrate so soon, I am not sure if you are the father to my baby.

 Oh no! Please tell me you are joking, please! I hope this is a joke. Diana please be serious with me.

 Tears drops out of Diana's eyes and runs through her cheeks. Her hearts becomes heavy, she feels pity for Oslow. Who father is it, if it's not me? He asks Diana. Your King, she says. You mean you have been sleeping with the King all these while. Wow now I get. He becomes more and More afraid. The king has been involved. What if the baby is for the king? What would Oslow do. I am not a prostitute, I don't sleep around for money. It was a huge mistake that I made and I wish I could reverse it. That night, the king lured me to his bed, and it all happened. I felt so guilty that I couldn't even stand you. I never expected it was going to end up like this. I am very sorry Oslow.

 She tells Oslow that the king is so excited about the pregnancy too. He wishes just as you so that this baby should be his. King silas has organized a pregnancy test to find out whom the child is for. As early as possible tomorrow, when it is dawn, the kingdom's physician will come and get me from the palace. Oslow I know I have done you wrong , but please forgive me please!!

Chapter 10

It is morning of the next day, the king has anxiously been waiting for dawn. Very early in the morning, the king leaves his chambers and goes to meet zampota the kingdom's physician. He tells him to get prepared for a test. He orders Kofi to go call Diana from her room, Kofi goes to Diana's room, he knocks on her door, she opens the door to him and greets him. He tells her that the king needs her attention. He wants her to do DNA test to prove the father of the baby. Diana didn't really want the test so soon but she has no choice, because the king was so anxious to know.

 She gets ready and follows Kofi to meet the king. They physician welcomes Diana. It is time for the test to commence, Oslow comes into the room and meets the Kofi, Diana and the King. He greets the king and Diana, he also was waiting for the test results and was also very anxious about it. He wanted to get the results as soon as possible. He is very convinced that the child is his.

 It is time for the test, the three of them enters with zampota, he took all his samples and tells them to wait outside. During the time of the test, zampota notices that the child Diana is carrying is for Oslow, he becomes confused about it, he finds it difficult to tell the king that Diana's child isn't him. He also expects the king to give him a lot of gifts and ornament if he tells the king that the child is his. He is in a state of dilemma. He decided to twist the results in favor of the King.

The long awaited hour has finally come. Zampota comes out of the room, King silas and Oslow stands up in haste. They needed to know who is the true father of the child. Zampota gives both of them the results. King Silas smiles profusely, he is so happy the results presented by zampota, shows that King Silas is the father of the Diana's child. Diana was happy that she now knows her son's father, but at the same time wasn't happy how she has treated Oslow. Oslow was so angry when he saw the test results. He didn't bother to say anything to anybody. He only tells Diana that he wishes her well. Diana is moved with pity, she is speechless, she doesn't know what she would have told Oslow. She begs him to forgive her, but he leaves in annoyance.

The king orders Kofi to brings gift, he have Zampota gifts and enough money, not knowing that he has changed the test results to favour the King.

The king rushes to the castle, he heads to his mother's room. On getting there, he says Mother, I have great news for you today. Guess what?

Silas, when were you going to tell me about it, you have kept it from me from a very long time and you think I wouldn't hear. When and how did you sleep with maiden? No only that you Impregnated her. After all the princess and beautiful girls I have showed you, you went on to take a maiden, your sisters maiden for that matter.

King Silas was a bit confused here, he tells Queen Issabella that she can no right to choose his Queen for him. He leaves her room angrily. And goes straight to his chambers.

While in his chambers he started thinking about what transpired, he remembers what the Wizard has prophesied and reflects on the remedy the old woman of Pampot had given to him.

He immediately orders for Diana. The palace guards calls Diana from her room. She see King silas in his room. He calls her to sit beside him, she does as he had asked. She sits beside him. She wonders why the king is requesting for her presence. He goes straight to the point this time. Diana are you a virgin? Angered by the question, she replies you should have known that when you have my legs on the air and fucked my pussy so hard. He apologizes for the question and asks her in a more pleasant manner. She gives him an answer this time. She tells him that she lost her virginity to her cousin. She explains the entire story of how she was raped when she was much younger. He was moved with pity and pets her, he apologizes for the episode that happened.

  He personally goes by night to meet Zampota, the kingdom's physician to clarify his results. Zampota out of fear for lying before, he keeps to his initial results and tells the king that the results are correct. The king trusts him and believes him. However, only Kofi and King silas knows about visit of the Old woman.

  The prophecy of the wizard is gradually coming to light.